I Can Read!

BEGINNING 1 READING

Syd Hoff's

DANNY AND THE DINOSAUR

Mind Their Manners

Written by Bruce Hale

Illustrated in the style of Syd Hoff by Charles Grosvenor

Color by David Cutting

HARPER

An Imprint of HarperCollins Publishers

One day, Danny and the dinosaur were walking to the museum when they saw a brand-new sign.

"What does that mean?"
asked the dinosaur.

"A king is a very important person,"
said Danny.

"And he's coming here!"

"Wow, I've never met royalty,"
said the dinosaur.
"What are kings like?"

"Kings are very fancy," said Danny.

"So if we want to meet a king,

we have to be on our best behavior."

"You mean say please and thank you?"
asked the dinosaur.

"Even more than that," said Danny.

"Maybe our manners need work."

"Tell me what to do,"

said the dinosaur.

"I can't wait to meet a king!"

Danny and the dinosaur bowed

to each other.

The dinosaur's bow needed

a little help.

Danny and the dinosaur

tried taking turns

using the drinking fountain.

Danny and the dinosaur worked on
standing up nice and straight.

The dinosaur stood up straighter.

The two pals washed their hands before eating.

MUSEUM

MEET THE KING

At lunch, Danny and the dinosaur

tried eating

with their mouths closed.

It was a little tricky at first,

but they managed.

"It's polite to compliment the cook
after a meal," said the
hot dog seller.

"That was delicious!"
said Danny and the dinosaur
together.

Danny and the dinosaur held the door

open for museum visitors.

"You're so polite," said one lady.

"Thank you, ma'am,"

said the dinosaur.

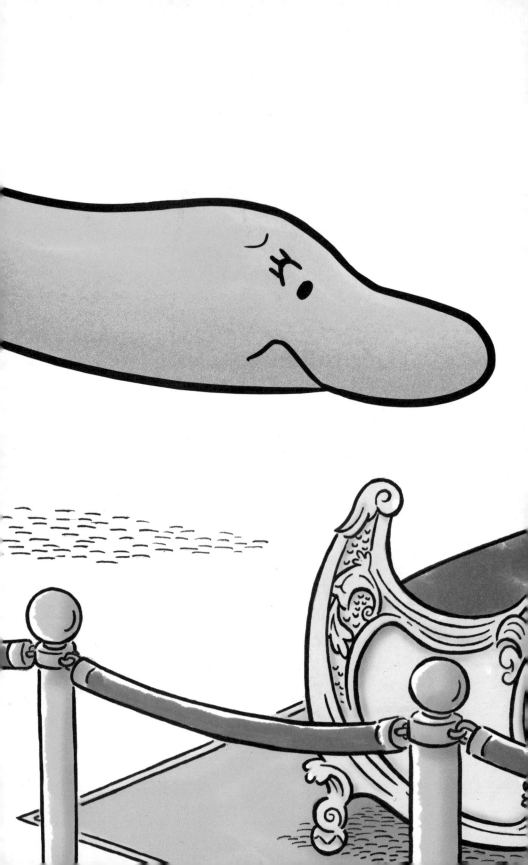

"What do you call a king, anyway?"
the dinosaur asked Danny.
"Mr. King? Your King-ness?"

"Let's ask the museum director,"
Danny said.

"You call him Your Majesty,"
said the museum director.

"Why do you ask?"

"We saw that a king is coming,
and we want to be polite
when we meet him," said Danny.

The director smiled.

"But this king isn't alive.

It's King Tut's mummy.

He died three thousand years ago."

Danny slumped.

The dinosaur looked sad.

All that hard work for nothing?

Then Danny looked up.

"Wait a minute," he said.

"A mummy? That's cool!"

"That's right," said the director.

"And you deserve a reward

for working so hard to be polite."

And when King Tut arrived,
guess who got to be
first in line?